Hooray for Sakai!
—S.P.

For my dear daughter, Amelia, and my husband, Jason,
whose love and support made this FEET possible.
—R.B-B.

Text copyright © 2005 by Susan Pearson
Pictures copyright © 2005 by Roxanna Baer-Block
All rights reserved
CIP Data is available.
Published in the United States 2005 by
Blue Apple Books
515 Valley Street, Maplewood, N.J. 07040
www.blueapplebooks.com
Distributed in the U.S. by Chronicle Books

First Edition
Printed in China
ISBN: 1-59354-093-0
1 3 5 7 9 10 8 6 4 2

Hooray for Feet!

Susan Pearson

Illustrations by Roxanna Baer-Block

BLUE APPLE BOOKS

Let's hear it for FEET!

They can't be beat.

Feet come in twos
in socks and shoes,

two boots with zippers,   two bunny slippers,

two swimming fins.

Feet are twins.

Fast

and slow feet.

Stop and go feet.

Feet play games—
they're just the thing
to jump a rope
or pump a swing.

They're also great
for running races—

but don't forget
to tie your laces.

Dancing feet—just think of those—

a hundred feet up on their toes

leaping, twirling, spinning, whirling,

hopping, bopping, never stopping.

When feet slow down,
they stroll or amble,

plod or dawdle,

mosey, ramble.

When feet speed up they're in a hurry!

Everyone knows that feet have toes.

Toes are good for counting ten,
playing piggies now and then,

painting toenails red or green,

good for squishing mud between

or curling on the sandy shore,

and tippytoeing on the floor.

Two feet,

ten toes—

HOORAY for those!

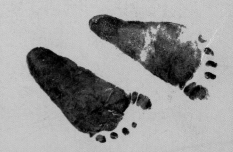